The Two Jacks

by

Tony Bradman

Illustrated by Ross Collins

D1386005

You do not need to read this page –
just get on with the book!

First published in 2002 in Great Britain by
Barrington Stoke Ltd
18 Walker Street, Edinburgh, EH3 7LP
www.barringtonstoke.co.uk

This edition first published in 2009

This edition based on *The Two Jacks*, published by
Barrington Stoke in 1999

ISBN: 978-1-84299-800-7

Printed in Great Britain by Bell & Bain Ltd

MEET THE AUTHOR — TONY BRADMAN

What is your favourite animal?
Whale
What is your favourite boy's name?
Thomas (my son's name)
What is your favourite girl's name?
Sally, Emma and Helen (my wife and
daughters)
What is your favourite food?
Grilled fish
What is your favourite music?
The Beatles
What is your favourite hobby?
Going to the cinema

MEET THE ILLUSTRATOR — ROSS COLLINS

What is your favourite animal?
Manatee
What is your favourite boy's name?
Connor
What is your favourite girl's name?
Wednesday
What is your favourite food?
Steak – medium rare
What is your favourite music?
Southern Swing
What is your favourite hobby?
Deep Sea pearl fishing

For Jacks and Miss Wilsons
everywhere

Contents

Chapter 1
Miss Wilson's First Day

This is the story of two boys called Jack, a new teacher called Miss Wilson and a small mistake that changed all of their lives.

The two Jacks lived in the same street and went to the same school. They were both in Mrs Heath's class and their names were almost the same.

Only one Jack had an extra 'r' in his name. One Jack was Jack BAKER and the other Jack was Jack *Barker*.

No-one ever mixed them up. For a start, they didn't look the same. Jack BAKER was small for his age. He had red hair and spoke in a soft voice. Jack *Barker* was big and dark and had a loud voice.

They didn't act the same either. You know how every class has the same types of people in it? There's the Joker and the Shy One and the Worrier and the Tell-Tale and the Boaster and the Chatterer and the Weirdo and the Two-Best-Friends-Who-Argue-All-The-Time.

Well, Jack BAKER was the Perfect Pupil and Jack *Barker* was the Naughty Boy. They had always been that way – or so one thought.

Jack BAKER was the boy who put his hand up first. He was the boy who got the right answer, the boy with top marks.

Jack Baker.

Jack Barker.

Teachers sent him to the office with the register. He was the polite boy who was asked to look after anyone important.

Jack *Barker* was nothing like that. He was the boy who never put his hand up, the boy who wouldn't do his work, the rude and cheeky boy who always behaved badly. He was the boy who had to be kept out of the way when anyone important came to visit the school.

The two Jacks didn't take much notice of each other. Jack BAKER was too busy being the Perfect Pupil, and Jack *Barker* was too busy being the Naughty Boy.

And that's how things would have gone on ... if it had not been for Miss Wilson.

Teachers come and teachers go.
Mrs Heath broke her leg playing football with the wild Year Six girls and she had to go to hospital.

So, Mrs Heath's class got a new teacher.

The new teacher was called Miss Wilson. When she came to school on her first morning, she felt quite nervous. She had begun to think that she wasn't much use as a teacher. She hadn't been able to get a full-time job and she was no good at keeping a class in order.

Maybe she was doing something wrong, she thought. She felt that she couldn't cope well in class. Did the children sense this? It was a worry to her. And it was getting worse.

"Ah, welcome to our school, Miss Wilson," said the Head and shook her hand. "I am so pleased to have you here. I didn't think we'd find anyone so soon. Now, let me show you round before the mob arrives and the battle begins. Just follow me ..."

The Head rushed Miss Wilson round the school. There was a lot for her to take in. He showed her the Hall, and the classrooms, and the staffroom. He told her where the tea and coffee and chocolate biscuits were kept. He showed her the teachers' toilets. Then the other teachers began to arrive.

The Head told her some of their names. Some teachers came up and told her who they were. Soon Miss Wilson's head was going round and round. Then it was time to go to the classrooms. She found herself running behind the Head to find hers.

"Er ... is there anything I should know about the class?" she said. The Head was marching down the corridor and it was hard to keep up. Miss Wilson could hear the children yelling in the playground. "Can I see their records?"

"Oh, they're a nice bunch," said the Head. "All the usual types. There's one perfect pupil, Jack BAKER, and one naughty boy, Jack *Barker*. Look out for those two. See you at lunchtime, if you're still alive then, ha ha!"

The Head strode off to his office and Miss Wilson went into her empty classroom.

Just then a whistle blew in the playground. The children stopped yelling and lined up to come in. She gave a gulp. Any moment now she would meet her class. What was it the Head had said? Look out for Jack BAKER and Jack *Barker*. One was the Perfect Pupil and one was the Naughty Boy. But she found it hard to remember which Jack was which.

Quick, quick, she thought, in a panic as she heard the children come into school. I must get it right. Yes, that was it. Jack *Barker* was the Perfect Pupil and Jack BAKER was the Naughty Boy. Phew, she thought, it was a good job she'd got *that* sorted out.

But we know that she'd got it wrong!

And *that* was the small mistake that changed all their lives.

Chapter 2
A Bit of a Mix-up

The children filed in and sat down. Jack BAKER came into the room first. He sat by the door because Mrs Heath liked to send him off with messages. Jack *Barker* came in last. His place was next to the teacher's desk so that she could keep an eye on him.

Everyone knew that Mrs Heath was away. They had this new teacher today, and that made things more interesting from the start. The children chatted softly to each other and just looked at Miss Wilson. They waited to see what kind of a teacher she was going to be.

"Good morning, everyone," said Miss Wilson. She sounded nervous.

"Good morning, Miss," said the class.

"My name is Miss Wilson," she went on, "and I'll be, er ... looking after you while Mrs Heath is away. I'm sorry but she'll be off for at least a week."

"She'll be all right, won't she?" said Kylie, the Worrier.

"Oh, I think so," said Miss Wilson gently. She knew what it was like to be someone who worried. "She just needs to get some rest. I think she's fine, apart from her leg, that is."

"It must be bad if she's apart from her leg, Miss," said Jamie, the Joker.

He giggled at his own joke and looked round at the rest of the class. A few of the other children giggled too. But most of them took no notice of him. They were looking at Miss Wilson to see what she would do next.

"Very funny," she said and smiled. So she wasn't going to be too strict. The class relaxed a bit.

In fact, *she* seemed nervous. "Well, let's get on," she said. "I had better begin by taking the register."

And so she took the register. She looked at each child in the class as they replied to their names. She studied the two Jacks more closely than the rest. At last she got to the end, made the last tick in the register and closed it up.

At once, Jack BAKER jumped up from his seat. "Shall I take it to the office, Miss?" he said.

"No, thank you, Jack," said Miss Wilson. He's the Naughty Boy, she thought.

"I'd like someone else to do it. I think I'll give it to the other Jack."

And she held the register out to Jack
Barker.

Everyone was looking at the register in
Miss Wilson's hand. A hush filled the room.
The children waited for something to
happen. She had asked Jack *Barker* to take
the register to the office and not Jack BAKER!
The Naughty Boy, not the Perfect Pupil!

It was as if the world had been turned upside down.

"Are you sure, Miss?" said Alice, the Tell-Tale. "Jack *Barker*'s ..."

"Sssh!" the other children hissed at her. The rest of the class knew Alice was about to tell Miss Wilson that this Jack was the Naughty Boy. They didn't want her to do that. The day was getting more and more interesting.

Luckily, Miss Wilson didn't seem to notice. "Quite sure," Miss Wilson said.

She would begin as she intended to go on. She would not allow anyone to argue with her. "Off you go, Jack *Barker*. I know I can trust you by looking at your face. The rest of us will start on some worksheets ..."

Jack *Barker* was amazed. He took the register from Miss Wilson and walked towards the door, as if he was in a dream. He stopped and looked back at Miss Wilson. She nodded to him, then carried on giving out the worksheets.

As Jack *Barker* passed Jack BAKER they looked at each other for a moment in shock. Then Jack *Barker* opened the door and Jack BAKER watched him sadly as he set off to the office.

"OK, has everybody got a worksheet?" Miss Wilson said. "Now listen all of you – and that means you too, Jack BAKER. Look at me, please."

Jack BAKER looked at her and went red in the face. Miss Wilson didn't sound cross with him. Mrs Heath never had to ask him to listen like that. He felt shocked.

Jack *Barker* was shocked too. He was amazed that Miss Wilson had asked *him* to go to the office. He was even more amazed

that he did take the register to the office
and came back to the class at once – well,
almost at once.

The class was acting in an odd way too. It was not just the two Jacks. Everyone was excited. Long before morning play, it was clear that Miss Wilson had got the two Jacks mixed up. She thought Jack BAKER was the Naughty Boy, and Jack *Barker* was the Perfect Pupil!

The children looked at each other and whispered some more. What were the two Jacks going to do next?

But before we find out, we need to know a bit more about them both.

Chapter 3
Jack BAKER's Story

Jack BAKER hadn't always been the Perfect Pupil. When he'd started school, he'd been just like the other little ones. Sometimes he was good, and sometimes he was naughty. Then his dad left home and didn't come back.

Jack was very small when his dad left. He didn't understand what was going on. All he knew was that his dad was there one

day, and the next he was gone. After that, Jack lived alone with his mum. But there was a great hole in his life.

Jack was very upset. He clung to his mum. He began to suck his thumb again. He wet the bed. And he kept asking when his dad was coming back. The answer was always the same – Dad wasn't coming back.

But Jack did still see him. For a time, his dad took him to the park, or out for a burger and chips on Saturdays. Then his dad missed one Saturday, and then the next one too. He went to work a long way away. But he did phone Jack when he could.

Then the phone calls stopped as well.

In the end, Jack didn't remember what his dad looked like. He gave up talking about him. He stopped sucking his thumb and wetting the bed.

On the outside, he was happy. He loved his mum and his mum loved him. She had a good job, they had a nice flat, and they had fun.

But on the inside – well, on the inside, it was not like that at all.

Jack did not *talk* about his dad, but he still *thought* about him a lot. What was he doing now? Why did he never send any birthday cards or Christmas presents? Why had his dad left home in the first place?

Jack knew his mum was very pretty. She was a great cook, she got on well with everyone and she was clever. Jack knew she was very good at her job, too. Jack made up his mind that his dad hadn't gone because of his mum.

He must have gone because of someone else.

Jack thought that it must have been because of *him* that his dad left. Was it something he had said, or done? Had he upset his dad? Maybe he hadn't been very good at his school work.

Jack had no idea what it was that had upset his dad and that worried him. What if his dad did come back and thought Jack was still letting him down? He'd leave home again. And what if Jack did something his mum didn't like? Would she go off too?

He made up his mind that he would just have to be perfect. He would make sure he did *nothing* wrong.

So, he helped his mum at home and worked hard at school. All the teachers said nice things about him. He liked that.

But he found out there was a dark side to being the Perfect Pupil. The other children were mean to him and called him 'boffin' and 'teacher's pet'.

And Jack felt he could never relax. He had to do his best all the time. Sometimes he did think it would be good not to worry so much. But he crushed that idea and worked even harder.

Then Miss Wilson came and turned his world upside down.

That morning, Jack had been keen to get off to a good start with the new teacher. But the day got worse and worse.

He had been shocked when he lost his register job and when Miss Wilson told him to listen. He had begun first to worry and then to panic. He never thought that Miss Wilson might have mixed him up with Jack *Barker*.

Jack BAKER was sure he must be doing something wrong. This made it hard for him to think about his work. When he handed in his worksheet, he hadn't done all the questions and he'd made some mistakes. The rest of the class was amazed.

As Jack went back to his seat, he was so upset that he didn't look where he was going.

He bumped into the teacher's desk and a vase of flowers fell to the floor and smashed. Jack looked down at the mess, then up at Miss Wilson.

She was cross. "Oh, Jack," she said, "you *are* naughty!"

Jack BAKER just didn't know what to say.

Chapter 4
Jack *Barker*'s Story

Jack *Barker* hadn't always been the Naughty Boy. When he'd started school with the other little ones, he'd been the same as them and Jack BAKER. In fact, he was quite good, and only a bit naughty.

But then his mum got ill.

Jack was very small at the time and he didn't understand what was going on.

He visited his mum in hospital but she couldn't speak to him.

Then one day his dad came home crying. Mum had died in the night. Jack didn't remember the funeral.

Like Jack BAKER, Jack had been very upset, but he didn't do the same kind of things. After the first few bad weeks, he became very silent. He worried that *he* might become ill and die, just like his mum.

He never told this to his dad. He didn't know how to. Anyway, his dad was very silent too. Then, after two or three months, his dad began to cheer up. And then his dad came home with a new friend – Jill, a lady from work.

Then, a year later, Jack's dad and Jill got married.

Jack had to dress up in fancy clothes for the wedding. He could remember running round a hall where there were lots of happy people. Jack was happy too, on the outside.

But on the inside ... it was not like that at all.

Jack never talked about his mum but he still thought about her most of the time. Often he wanted to talk about her to his dad. But he didn't think his dad would like it. He had a new wife now. Deep down, Jack was angry with his dad and his step-mum.

He began to be naughty with them, and most of all with his step-mum. At first, she tried not to get cross. Then she had a baby, a little girl. And then she had two more baby girls. This made life hard for Jack.

Babies are lovely and Jack was fond of his little sisters. But his dad and his step-mum were very busy and worn out. They didn't have much time for Jack. He was a bit clumsy, and once or twice he bumped into a baby's chair or hugged a little sister too hard.

Here we go again

He didn't mean to hurt them. But he still got told off. That made him feel even more angry with his dad and his step-mum. He became even more naughty, first at home and then at school as well. Everyone was cross with him.

The more he was told off, the more naughty he became. Soon everyone, and Jack too, had forgotten that he had ever been good.

From time to time, he heard teachers saying horrid things about him. Jack pretended not to care. He had found out that it paid off to be a Naughty Boy. It was a good way to make sure you got plenty of attention.

Jack also liked to impress the other kids. He did sometimes think it would be nice if the teachers liked him. But he crushed that idea and went on being naughty.

Then Miss Wilson came and turned his world upside down.

Jack hadn't been interested in her that morning. He'd just thought she might give him a hard time, like his other teachers.

But the day got more and more amazing. He had been shocked when he was asked to do the register job. Miss Wilson had said she knew she could trust him *just by looking at his face*!

On the way back from the office, he slipped into the boys' toilets to look at his face in the mirror.

Could Miss Wilson see something everyone else had missed?

****

Back in class, he sat and looked at his worksheet. Jack's way of doing worksheets was to draw rude pictures on them and not to answer the questions. But he couldn't do that with Miss Wilson. He did his best to finish it.

When Jack BAKER knocked the vase over and was told off by Miss Wilson, Jack *Barker* put up his hand. Miss Wilson turned and smiled.

"Don't worry, Miss!" said Jack *Barker*. "I'll clear it up for you!"

"Oh, Jack," she said, "you *are* good!"

Chapter 5
Miss Wilson Works it Out

There was silence for a moment. Nobody knew what to say.

Then Miss Wilson nodded to Jack *Barker*. She told Jack BAKER to help him.

Soon the two Jacks were picking up the bits of the smashed vase and the flowers. They dumped the lot in her bin.

Miss Wilson thanked Jack *Barker* and told Jack BAKER to be more careful. Both Jacks went back to their seats.

"OK, everyone, I think we'll do some maths. What book do you use?"

And so the morning went by. Miss Wilson thought things were going well. The class wasn't as bad as other classes she'd had and she relaxed a bit. She felt she had sorted the children out.

It was going to be OK, Miss Wilson told herself. But just before lunchtime, she began to worry again. The class was almost too quiet. The children seemed excited, almost as if they were hoping something was going to happen at any moment.

And the two Jacks were a puzzle.

Jack BAKER had knocked over the vase but was that just bad luck? He hadn't done anything else that was naughty.

Then there was his worksheet. It had been neat and tidy, and he'd got more questions right than anyone else. It was odd that he'd been upset when he'd made a few mistakes.

Jack *Barker* had offered to clear up the mess when the vase broke. But everyone else in the class had been amazed. That was odd if he was the Perfect Pupil.

Then there was Jack *Barker's* worksheet. It had been messy and he'd got most of the questions wrong. But he'd seemed so happy when he'd handed it in. It was as if he felt pleased to have done anything at all.

Miss Wilson was still thinking how odd this was when the bell went for lunch.

Most of the children went off, but Jack
BAKER hung back. He looked unhappy.

Jack *Barker* was still there too and asked
if he could do anything for her.

"Er ... no, I don't think so," she said. "You
two boys run along."

There was a lot going on in the staffroom. Teachers were making tea and coffee. They were eating their lunch and telling each other about the awful things that had happened that morning.

Miss Wilson found a seat in the corner and started to eat her own packed lunch.

"You're still with us then, Miss Wilson, ha ha!" said the Head, standing right beside her. "And it seems you've made a fine start. I don't know what you've done to Jack *Barker*. They told me in the office he was as good as gold when he came in with the register. Keep up the good work!"

Miss Wilson did not know what to think. She forgot about her lunch. The Head seemed to think that Jack *Barker* was the Naughty One!

Miss Wilson began to think she might have made a small·mistake.

By the end of lunch, she *knew* she'd got it wrong. She had talked to the other teachers in the staffroom and found out that they all had tales about the naughty things Jack *Barker* had done. And they only had nice things to say about Jack BAKER.

Miss Wilson walked sadly back to her classroom. She felt she was no good as a teacher. How could she have been so stupid? How could she have got the two Jacks mixed up?

The whistle blew in the playground and there was a hush outside.

Miss Wilson had an idea. She knew that she'd upset Jack BAKER – but her mistake had made Jack *Barker* behave well for a change.

Maybe the mix-up hadn't been such a bad thing after all.

Chapter 6
A Fresh Start

That afternoon was not as much fun as they had hoped. Miss Wilson soon made it clear that she *hadn't* got the two Jacks mixed up any more. She smiled at Jack BAKER and let him be her helper. She was more worried about Jack *Barker* now.

It seemed that the world was turning the right way up again.

Jack BAKER felt much better, but still felt worried. He worked even harder to impress Miss Wilson. And Jack *Barker* felt very mixed up. From now on, was Miss Wilson going to treat him just the same as every other teacher did?

They were both in for a surprise. Miss Wilson stayed on after school that day. She went to the office and asked for the class records. She wanted to find out as much as she could about the two Jacks.

She studied the records with care. The next day, she asked the other teachers lots of questions. She had begun to see that there was a lot to learn about Jack BAKER and Jack *Barker.* Both of them had a problem in their past life.

It had been very hard for Jack *Barker* when he lost his mum. Then a new stepmum and three baby sisters arrived. Jack BAKER became so worried about being perfect that he was never able to relax or have any fun.

Everyone expected Jack *Barker* to be naughty and Jack BAKER to be perfect, she thought. No-one let them be any different. But someone must give them a chance. Miss Wilson made up her mind that she would be the person to do it. She started with Jack *Barker.*

"Hang on, Jack," she said as the other children went for lunch. "Could I have a word?"

"Yes, Miss?" Jack said. He stopped by her desk, with a frown on his face. He didn't think he had done anything naughty but he waited to be told off.

"I need someone to be paper monitor for the rest of the week," said Miss Wilson. "Would *you* like to do the job?"

"Er ... *me*, Miss?" said a stunned Jack.

"Yes, *you*, Jack," she said and smiled. "Don't look so shocked. Well, what do you say?"

"Thanks, Miss!" said Jack with a huge grin. "I won't let you down!"

That afternoon and for the next few days, Jack *Barker* was the best paper monitor the class had seen. He was grateful to Miss Wilson for giving him the job. He tried hard at his work, too.

Not that he became the Perfect Pupil. Jack had been naughty for so long that he couldn't change just like that. But everyone in the school noticed that he was a lot less naughty these days. And even when he *was* naughty, he was more cheeky and funny than really bad.

Sorting Jack BAKER out was harder.

Miss Wilson tried to get him to relax and not to worry about being perfect. But it didn't work. Then, on her third day with the class, she heard Jack *Barker* being cheeky to a teacher and she had an idea.

"Hang on, Jack," she said to Jack BAKER as the children left at the end of school. "Could I have a word?"

"Yes, Miss?" said Jack, looking worried as he stopped by the door. He didn't think he'd done anything wrong.

"I'd like you to sit next to Jack *Barker* tomorrow, Jack," she said. "You'll be able to help me more if you're sitting closer to my desk."

"Will I, Miss?" said Jack looking rather more happy.

"Yes, Jack," said Miss Wilson and smiled. "I think it'll do you good to be near someone who knows how to have fun. And, one more thing. Don't worry, OK?"

"No, Miss," said Jack, not sure about that at all. "I'll try not to."

The next day, Miss Wilson could see that putting the two Jacks next to each other was going to help them both. Jack BAKER could help Jack *Barker* with his school work, and Jack *Barker* could help Jack BAKER to relax and enjoy life a little more. It still wouldn't be easy for either of them.

Miss Wilson wished she could stay longer in the school. But this was her last day. She had to go just when she had begun to help the two Jacks. She was feeling better about her teaching, too.

Then the classroom door opened and in came the Head. "Ah, Miss Wilson," he said. "It seems Mrs Heath will be off for a while yet with her broken leg. Could you stay on here till the end of term – or even longer? And did I tell you Mrs Heath is going to leave at the end of this year anyway?

Miss Wilson looked at the two Jacks and smiled, and they smiled back.

Sometimes things in life, just as in stories, really do work out OK.

Swop!
by
Hilary McKay

Can Emily swop her horrible home for a
happy ending?
Emily love swops. She even swops her gran
for a donkey! But can her swops save her and
her brother from wicked old Aunty Bess?

You can order *Swop! 4u2read edition* from our website at
www.barringtonstoke.co.uk

Grow Up, Dad!

by

Narinder Dhami

Be careful what you wish for –
you might just get it!
Robbie feels like his dad doesn't understand
him. Until one day, with a bit of magic, his
dad finds himself in Robbie's shoes. And
Robbie's in his dad's! How will they cope?

You can order *Grow Up, Dad! 4u2read edition* from our
website at www.barringtonstoke.co.uk